BEGINNINGS
and ENDINGS

A SELECTION OF SHORT STORIES

BOOKS BY JANE SUEN

Children of the Future

Flowers in December

Alterations

Beginnings and Endings: A Selection of Short Stories

BEGINNINGS
and ENDINGS

A SELECTION OF SHORT STORIES

JANE SUEN

BEGINNINGS AND ENDINGS: A Selection Of Short Stories

Jane Suen books are available for order through Ingram Press Catalogues

www.janesuen.com

Printed in the United States of America

First Printing: November 2017

Paperback ISBN: 978-0-9979297-6-8

Hardback ISBN: 978-0-9979297-8-2

E-book ISBN: 978-0-9979297-7-5

For the child we were and the child we have.

TABLE OF CONTENTS

1

GRITS GIRL

"How fast can you say 'scattered, smothered, covered'?" Eric asked.

I gulped my coffee and set it on the counter. "How fast can *you* say it?" I teased as I picked apart the hash on my plate, wishing I'd added the diced tomatoes. I was famished, so I'd ordered the hash on top of my usual bowl of grits.

Girl, I love my grits! A satisfied "mmm" escaped my lips as another spoonful slid down my throat.

Eric laughed. He was busy digging into his scrambled eggs. "That good, huh?"

"Uh huh," I managed to mumble. The cook outdid himself today. I glanced toward the grill, seeking him out. I raised my mug, mouthing, "Compliments to the chef."

We were seated at the counter, right up close to the action. I liked to watch and listen, especially when the hustle and bustle of a busy kitchen filled the air; the clinking dishes and shouted orders mixed with the sizzle and snap of food cooking.

"You been to the new café next to the fancy boutique?" I asked.

Eric shook his head. "You?"

"Yeah, I went to try out their grits. They had the cheesy kind." I crinkled my nose.

"Don't like those?"

"Nah. Too cheesy."

"You're picky."

"No kidding," I said.

"And?"

"I always come back here …" I smiled, thinking back to that day almost two years ago.

We were both students then, struggling to make ends meet. After a marathon study session at the library, our group quickly dissipated, leaving the two of us standing outside on the steps. I lingered for a moment. I admit I was a bit curious about Eric, a quiet guy who seemed serious and polite.

He broke the silence. "Hungry?"

"Starved."

He shuffled his backpack, shifting his weight. "What do you like to eat?"

"Grits," I said without hesitation. I could see it took him by surprise, and I imagined him thinking absurdly, *At this time of the night?*

He recovered quickly and smiled. "I know just the place. Breakfast 24/7 and all the grits you can eat."

That night, I had my grits and we talked for hours

until the predawn morning. We were high on caffeine, supplied by a perky, rail-thin waitress named "Belle" with her ever-ready coffee refills. It was a slow night at the diner, with only the grill cook and waitress working.

We managed to come back every week thereafter. It became a tradition, our tradition. In between our visits, I'd try out all the new cafés, always comparing their meals to this place … our homey place with its plain, unpretentious grits.

"I remember," whispered Eric, his warm breath tickling my ear.

I turned to him, seeking out the familiar parts of his face—the dark curls sweeping over his brow, the faint lines creasing when he frowned and when he smiled, the intense brown eyes. I reached out to trace his jawline.

He caught my fingers, enveloping my petite hand in the warmth of his palm. Content and happy, I savored the moment. He leaned in to give me a kiss. As our kiss broke, I opened my eyes. He was grinning a happy, silly grin.

"You know how many times we've been here?"

I hadn't been counting, but ran a quick estimate in my head.

"Our one-hundredth time today," he blurted out, before I could answer.

"Every week for almost two years," I murmured.

"Here." He carefully placed a small, painted wooden box on the counter in front of me.

"What's this?"

"Something I made …"

I squealed with delight, running my fingers over the beautiful, pale-blue whitewash, feeling the smooth surface. "It's lovely!"

Pleased, Eric smiled. Tapping the clasp, he said, "Open it."

"Oh." I gasped as I popped open the lid. I stared at the ring inside, a tiny diamond the size of a pencil tip perched on top.

"Will you—?" he asked with a quaver in his voice, stopping in mid-sentence.

I tore my eyes away from the ring, locking my gaze with his.

"Will you marry me?"

"Oh Eric—" I hesitated, my mouth forming a silent "O" while my mind wandered, charting a path running through meadows and brooks, crossing hills and valleys, going up and down and around. I saw myself on the path, walking, at times stumbling, falling and getting up again. I wasn't alone, but I couldn't see the face of the man who was beside me.

He shifted slightly, clearing his throat. "Um …"

I caught sight of the sparkle in his eyes, gentle yet strong, shining bright and bathing me with love. My heart fluttered. Will he love me when I'm old and wrinkled, or sick? Will he be there, when I'm down, to pick me up? Will it be Eric and me, taking this journey together? I went back to the path, searching for answers.

"Our one-hundredth time here," I mumbled, my memories taking me back to the beginning when I first met him and the times since then. My thoughts seemed to run through my head for an eternity, but it was only a few seconds. My hand strayed to pluck a piece of lint on my jeans, idling there. And, in that moment, I knew. Here, in my favorite grits place, the man I was looking for—a man with true grit—was right beside me.

I smiled. "Yes!" I repeated it, shouting "YES!", as he slid the ring on my finger.

2

THE ACCIDENT

S he woke up in a sweat.

A loud sound had jolted her awake and left her trembling with fear. What was that? A gun? A bomb? Her mind was frantic. She remembered her dream—the horror of reliving it—a charging chunk of metal coming at her out of nowhere, hitting the car, thrusting it into oncoming traffic, careening out of control. It happened so fast. *Wait! Stop! What the heck just happened?* One moment it was a beautiful day—the next second, everything changed.

Adeline's nightmare always stopped there, lingering at the intersection where her fate had hung in the air. She grasped her cotton nightshirt tighter over her chest, calming herself. She didn't need this. She pulled herself up and swung her legs over the bed. Her feet touched the cool planks of the pine floor before finding her slippers. Shivering, she grabbed the sweater slung over the bedroom chair.

She made her way down the hall to the bathroom.

The face in the mirror looked tired, with dark shadows under her large hazel eyes. She pressed her unpainted lips firmly together and brushed aside the wisps of damp hair clinging to her forehead. Adeline studied each feature. Taken by itself, each was ordinary. Yet when it was all put together, the face became extraordinary, interesting … and possessed a haunting beauty.

Turning on the faucet of the bathroom sink, Adeline let the water run until it warmed and dipped her facecloth in, cupping it as the weight of the wet fabric expanded. When it was hot enough, she turned off the water and wrung the cloth. Burying her face in it, the tension evaporated as her muscles relaxed.

Mornings were the worst. Adeline flicked off the bathroom light. She glanced back at the bed.

With a sigh, she shuffled to the kitchen to start a pot of coffee. She had bought a new canister, a robust, dark, organic blend from the hills of Sumatra. Digging the scoop into the rich grind, she inhaled the delightful aroma. While it brewed, Adeline slid a pat of butter into the frying pan for the omelet. She chopped spinach, bell peppers, baby bella mushrooms and onions. As they sautéed in the pan, she scrambled the eggs. The chef at the deli had taught her how to make a quick omelet, using two pans, keeping them both hot. She smiled, remembering how he had added an extra grab of spinach leaves, knowing she liked it.

Adeline set the dining room table for two. Pleased with herself, she surveyed it before wiping her hands on the kitchen towel and heading back to the bedroom.

As she gently shook the sleeping figure, she whispered his name. "Stuart."

He groaned. It wasn't the sound of a man still groggy from too much sleep. It was different now. The groans barely masked the pain that no amount of sleep could relieve.

"Breakfast is ready." She tugged at his arm.

"Thanks," Stuart said as he met her eyes. A glint of appreciation flashed, before it disappeared, replaced by pain, frustration, anger and a mixture of apologetic shame and resentment.

He had faced the toughest situations in Afghanistan. He had wanted to go there. He did the first tour and returned in one piece. Later, they offered a nice bonus if he signed up for another tour. She didn't want him to go again. He did it for her, to buy her this house, their home. They got married before he left. She had prayed for him and was overjoyed when he came back to her unharmed.

Why did he survive only to be dealt this cruel blow?

It was difficult for him to talk about what happened in the war, his feelings of worthlessness now. Stuart was a proud man. Confronted with the hard reality of being dependent on Adeline, knowing he couldn't be the man she married—this was, for him, the hardest thing to accept.

It took awhile, as Adeline knew it would. Today she had patience, but she was ashamed of the days she didn't, when she blamed him and only thought of herself, how much trouble it was for her. Remorse always followed. And regret.

Stuart relied on his arms to lift himself out of his wheelchair. Adeline pulled back the dining table chair, so Stuart could flop into it from his seat. Everything took much longer. His lips pursed. Adeline clasped her hands behind her, knowing he wanted to do this on his own.

She was there. Stuart had been driving the car and it was no fault of his. The other driver came out of nowhere, speeding recklessly, charging across lanes of traffic in a rush to make the exit ramp, ramming his truck into their vehicle.

Adeline had lashed out at Stuart, desperation mounting amidst the fear as she watched him lying there helplessly, his body twisted. Stuart had been so strong, so fearless. He had traveled across the globe and survived Afghanistan to come home safely to her—only to be hurt in a car accident.

Pushing away the bitterness, Adeline searched for the good memories. They were still there. She remembered their first kiss and the sweet promise of more, the porch swing creaking as they sat and gazed upon the wondrous full moon, the warmth of his arms encircling her as she shivered in the cold, her delight in the goofy Halloween costume he made for her out of his old shirt.

She smiled, cherishing the happy times, the laughter, what they had together ... and found her way back to the love supporting her backbone. Adeline stood up straighter.

When he was seated, she poured his coffee.

3

THE END OF SUMMER

"Where you headed?"

I tucked a thick lock behind my ear, wishing these strays would stay put. I leaned forward, peering through the half-open window of the dirt-streaked station wagon. A pleasant-looking man with sandy hair in his late twenties or early thirties looked back.

"East," I said, tossing my thumb toward the highway. "I want to get to Virginia at some point."

"I'm heading in that direction." He paused. "I could take you as far as the western part of the state."

I noticed the guy looking at me as I glanced at the back seat, my eyes widening as I caught a glimpse of a foot sticking out from under the blanket.

"My kid's back there, sleeping," he said with a loving smile. He tilted his head. "C'mon, hop in the front."

I slipped my well-traveled backpack off my shoulders and opened the car door. "Thanks, man."

"You can toss your stuff in the back. Give yourself more room."

"I'm Tim," I said, settling into the passenger seat and stretching out my legs.

"I'm Mike, and the kid is Mike Junior." He paused, and continued quietly. "We didn't get to name him in time, so it was Mike Junior. Mikey is his nickname."

"Mikey," I repeated. *Does he look like his father?*

Mike checked the highway and looked over his shoulder as he sped up to get back on the road. His hand tugged at his seatbelt absentmindedly.

"How about some music?" he asked.

I hesitated and glanced back at the kid.

"Oh, Mikey is used to the radio. He can sleep through it."

I nodded.

Keeping his eyes on the road, Mike fumbled with the radio dial and turned it on, settling on, "Everything I Own" by Bread. *Oh, how I love this song! No matter how many times I've listened to it, the music still moves me.*

I looked out the window. We were leaving Indiana, heading southeast toward the Ohio border. I never knew land could be so flat, the horizontal line of dark earth stretching as far as the eye could see.

"So what brought you out here?" Mike asked as the song ended.

"Summer job. I worked on a ranch out west."

"Really?"

"Yeah. I wanted to try my hand at something different." I laughed. "Errrrr, as a ranch hand."

"Did you like it?"

"Well, not at first. I had a lot to learn. It was hard work, long hours. I was the low man on the totem pole."

Mike uttered a sympathetic grunt.

"Honestly, I didn't like shoveling manure."

"Mucking the stalls, huh?"

"Yep."

"Heading back east for school?"

"Not yet, I'm taking some time off to figure things out."

"How old are you?

"Nineteen."

"You've got your whole life ahead of you." Mike paused. "I met Mikey's mom when I was your age. It was the '60s … wild, crazy time. Marlina, she was so beautiful and spirited. I was drawn to her in ways I couldn't comprehend."

"You loved her?"

"Oh God, yes. She was my soul mate, my everything."

"Where is she now? I'd like to meet her," I blurted out.

I felt a tug as the kid leaned forward in the back, his fingers gripping the top of my seat, slightly pulling it. He wiped a little dribble of saliva from the corner of his lip before he spoke. "Who're you?" he asked, eyeing me with interest.

"Hey, Mikey," I said, turning around to face him. The car seat seam had pressed a faint imprint onto his cheek. "I'm Tim," I said with a smile. "I hitched a ride with your dad while you were sleeping."

Mike turned down the radio to talk to Mikey. "Hey kid, you sleep well?"

"Yeah, Dad," Mikey answered with another yawn. "Where are we now?"

"We've crossed the line to Ohio. You want to check the map?"

I could hear the crackle of paper as Mikey opened a map of the eastern United States and unfolded it. His fingers traced the highway across the state as he scrunched his brow to decipher the lettering and numbers. With an impatient shake, he quickly folded the map. He rifled through the stuff in the back until he triumphantly whipped out another, this time of the northeastern United States.

I craned my neck to look. Mikey had his finger on a spot circled in pencil. It looked like some words were scrawled next to it. I saw another circle in red ink, further southeast, with a star next to it.

"Hey, Dad, how much longer until we get there?"

"Should be about another hour or so. You help me with signs."

Pleased, Mikey eased closer to the window to get a better look.

Mike turned to me. "We are going to make a stop soon, a little detour. You okay with that?"

I threw him a look. "Where?"

"I made a promise to Mikey," Mike explained. "He's been looking forward to it—his first time at the fair—the midway with the carnival rides, food, games, fun ..."

Mikey made an excited noise.

I had been a kid myself not so long ago. I knew the feeling. But my experience was tinged with the bittersweet memory of my first county fair. I had saved up every bit of money I made in the summer from cutting grass and doing odd jobs. It wasn't much. A nickel here, a dime there, sometimes a quarter. But it all added up. By the time the carnival rolled into town at the end of summer, I had a whopping ten dollars in my piggy bank. I'd gone to the bank and turned in my change for a brand-new ten-dollar bill.

When the big day came, I woke up early after tossing and turning all night. The excitement of the carnival permeated the small town. Folks came from all over, arriving in cars and trucks. Kids with eyes as big as dollar coins ogled at the rides and fought over which ones they could ride, stretching to look tall so they could pass the mark on the measuring stick. Colorful lights were strewn all over the place. Little kids not old enough to ride were closely watched by their parents lest they dash away.

I had planned it all out, which rides I'd go on, how I'd stretch out my money for a whole day of fun. In the morning, I gulped down my breakfast of cereal and milk and carefully placed my ten-dollar bill in my wallet, pushing it deep down into the pocket of my jeans.

With my hard-earned money, I walked under the banner into the wonderland of carnival fun. I detected a trace of pride in my dad's eyes. The stream of people pushed us toward the edges where I could see the first tents. I heard the carny men shouting above the noise of the crowd. As we moved closer, one of them caught sight of me and waved me over to his tent, all the while talking like a crazed man at an auction. I stood in front of his booth looking at the display of small toys and stuffed animal prizes. He pointed at the balls in a bushel basket, grabbed one of them and demonstrated throwing it. It looked like an easy toss.

"How much?" I heard myself asking.

"Fifty cents, you get six tries."

Still I hesitated.

"A quarter, you get three!"

Okay, that got me. I reached into my pocket and pulled out my ten-dollar bill. The man peeled off nine one-dollar bills from a big roll of money, and dug into his pockets for the change. My dad was silent, watching the transaction, allowing me to do this on my own. It was my choice how I'd spend my hard-earned money.

I threw the first ball and missed. Ten minutes later I finally turned away from the tent, my pockets empty. Before I'd even had any fun, I had lost my entire fortune on that old crooked carny game.

Mikey poked me in the arm. He could barely contain his excitement. I looked at him, not willing to burst his bubble. Maybe he'd have a better first time.

When we pulled into the parking lot, the fair was in full swing. We were lucky to find a spot right at the edge under a big oak tree. I saw cars piled with kids, fresh-faced and eager. I could see the big Ferris wheel in the distance. We quickly gathered our things and made plans. I decided I'd stick with them. If we got separated, we would meet back at the station wagon.

My stomach was grumbling, so I announced, "Hot dogs for everyone. I'm buying." This brought a smile from both father and son. I led the way to the food stands, maneuvering quickly past the little tents at the front of the carnival where the games of skill teased the unsuspecting crowd.

Mikey had some money saved up from his paper route, but big Mike had told his son to leave his money in the car, mumbling something about keeping it safe.

The memory of my first carnival lingered on, leaving a trace of anger. I could still see the carny's grubby fingers peeling off bills from his thick roll of money, his fingernails darkened with dirt. What kind of man would prey on unsuspecting little kids to take their money? If I saw that grimy man with stubble on his chin and greasy hair today, I'd punch him out. But then again, maybe I'll keep my hands clean.

I was determined to enjoy myself and do my best so Mikey's first fair would be the idyllic one I never had. I stuffed my mouth full of hot dogs before we headed toward the rides. Mikey was too fired up to eat. Soon he was screaming with laughter as we spun around and around in the Tilt-A-Whirl, the three of us riding together in a car. By the time we stopped, I could barely hold myself together. I stumbled out, my stomach churning with the hot dogs.

I retched up my lunch and sat out the next few rides, which were two-seaters, and perfect for the two of them. I didn't mind watching.

Mikey finally persuaded me to join them on the Dodgem, so I got into a lemon-colored bumper car. We sat in our cars along a circular track, waving at each other as we started moving.

"Watch out!" shouted Mikey as his car careened into mine.

"Whoa!" I squeaked, trying to turn my wheels to avoid smashing into Mike, who was running neck and neck with a car driven by a chubby red-headed boy with the most determined look on his face.

Everyone was bumping into each other and turning this way and that, seemingly at about five miles per hour. "Faster, faster," I goaded. As much as I prodded my car, it refused to go much faster. The "race" was to see how many bumper cars you could ram. Or, how many cars you could dodge. I laughed so hard. We ended up going on the Dodgem again. And again.

We capped off the night with a ride on the merry-go-round, all lit up with bright lights and loud music blaring. I couldn't help being a bit silly. But no one was paying any attention. We picked horses in a row and sat, enjoying the ride. Afterward, Mikey said he wanted a big swirl of pink cotton candy. He'd never had one before. It was amusing to watch him take a big bite out of it, clamping his teeth to tear a morsel while strings of gooey cotton candy stuck on his cheeks and his nose.

My journey had intersected with theirs and I found solace, putting to rest my childhood.

I took another detour on that ride east. It's one I remember as clearly.

We stood in front of an apple tree. I wasn't aware Mike had been crying until I heard his soft sobs and saw his cheeks wet with tears. I waited until he finally spoke.

"We lived on this farm, in communal living. We worked the land, grew our food, raised chickens. We were pretty much self-sufficient." He paused, speaking his next words so softly I had to lean forward to catch them. "When Marlina found out she was pregnant, she wanted to have a home birth—a natural birth." His voice broke, and he caught his breath before he went on. "But after she had the baby, something went wrong … we couldn't save her. She was so brave." He struggled to continue. "She made me promise to bury her placenta here after she died, and to plant a fruit tree." He knelt to touch the earth underneath the apple tree, running his fingers gently over the soil, brushing away a small rock.

"I'm sorry," I said, my hand reaching out to offer comfort.

"You know how long I've been away?"

"How long?"

"Eleven years. Ever since Mikey was born." His eyes sought mine before he continued. "This is the first time I've brought him back."

Mikey's yell sounded in the distance. "Hey, c'mon!

Let's go feed the horses!" He was already down the hill to the pasture, waving an apple. He had stayed only long enough to pluck one.

"Have you told him yet?" I asked.

He shook his head. "This trip, this is why we came. I wanted to wait until Mikey was old enough."

"Is it time?"

Mike stood up, watching as Mikey held out the apple to the horse. The horse stepped closer, stretching its neck out. "It's time," he said.

The ~~End~~
Beginning

BONUS

PICK ME

E very day, the best and finest get picked. I'm in a better position today than yesterday. In front, right at the top, dead center. Full exposure. If this doesn't do it, I don't know what will. Confident, I glance at my competitors. *Ha! They don't have a chance.*

I'm so tired of being ogled, manhandled and checked out like a piece of meat. *Hey, I'm not a piece of meat, you bugger! Is it perfection that you seek?*

I hear voices. Coming closer. A slight squeak of wheels. Suddenly I am snatched up.

"Mommy, this one!" a little girl shrieks, blowing a blast of warm breath my way.

"Honey, put it down!"

"I pick today," she insists and pouts, still holding on to me. "You prooomised!"

Mommy tries to grab me out of the little girl's hands. "Let me see it!"

"No! I tell you it's perrrfect..." says the little girl as she clutches me.

"Did you do the squeeze test, Ava?"

Hot little fingers tighten on me. *Oh, I prefer the tiny hands. The big hands … sometimes they squeeze so hard it hurts. They don't know their own strength.*

Yesterday I was handled so many times I lost count. Yet not a single person picked me. *Too hard. Not ready. Don't pick that one.*

A pair of large brown eyes peers at me. Experienced, adult eyes! Mommy's mouth opens, framed by lips the color of red grapes. "Well, well, what do we have here?" She touches me with deft fingers.

I gulp. *Oh oh, here we go again!*

Then the eyes crinkle with the smile. "Ava, you picked the best avocado!"